Joe's Wish

James Proimos

Harcourt Brace & Company

San Diego   New York   London

For Michelle

Requests for permission to make copies of any part of the work should be mailed to: Permissions Department, Harcourt Brace & Company, 6277 Sea Harbor Drive, Orlando, Florida 32887-6777.

Library of Congress Cataloging-in-Publication Data
Proimos, James.
Joe's wish/by James Proimos.
p. cm.
Summary: More than anything, an old man wishes he were young again—until he spends the day with his grandson.
ISBN 0-15-201831-X
[1. Old age—Fiction. 2. Grandfathers—Fiction.
3. Wishes—Fiction.] I. Title.
PZ7.P9432Jo 1998
[E]—dc21 97-40837

First edition

A C E F D B

Printed in Mexico

The illustrations in this book were first drawn with a pen,
then colorized in Adobe Photoshop.
The display type was set in Fontesque.
The text type was set in Goudy Old Style.
Color separations by Bright Arts Ltd., Hong Kong
Printed and bound by RR Donnelley & Sons, Reynosa, Mexico
This book was printed on totally chlorine-free
Nymolla Matte Art paper.
Production supervised by Stanley Redfern and Ginger Boyer
Designed by Kaelin Chappell and James Proimos

Joe Capri stared into the night, through the clouds, and wished on a star.

Joe was mighty old.

His legs were tired.

His skin was
wrinkled.

And when he bent
down, he creaked.

So he wished a wish that was older than
he was.

"Please," he begged, "I want to be young
again."

That night, when Joe went to bed, his head was filled with dreams of his boyhood days.

He slept like a baby until, at break of day, the sun spilled through his bedroom window and spoiled everything.

"I'm still the very same guy I was before I went to bed," Joe lamented as he shaved his perfectly wrinkled face. "What's the use of wishing, anyway?"

And with that Joe turned his thoughts to breakfast.

If there was one thing Joe Capri relished, it was breakfast.

He loved waffles topped with whipped cream, blueberry pancakes drenched in maple syrup, scrambled eggs smothered in ketchup—you name it.

Just as he sat down to eat, there
was a knock on the door, and before
he could answer it, a quite amazing

Something or Other

appeared before him.

The Something or Other had...

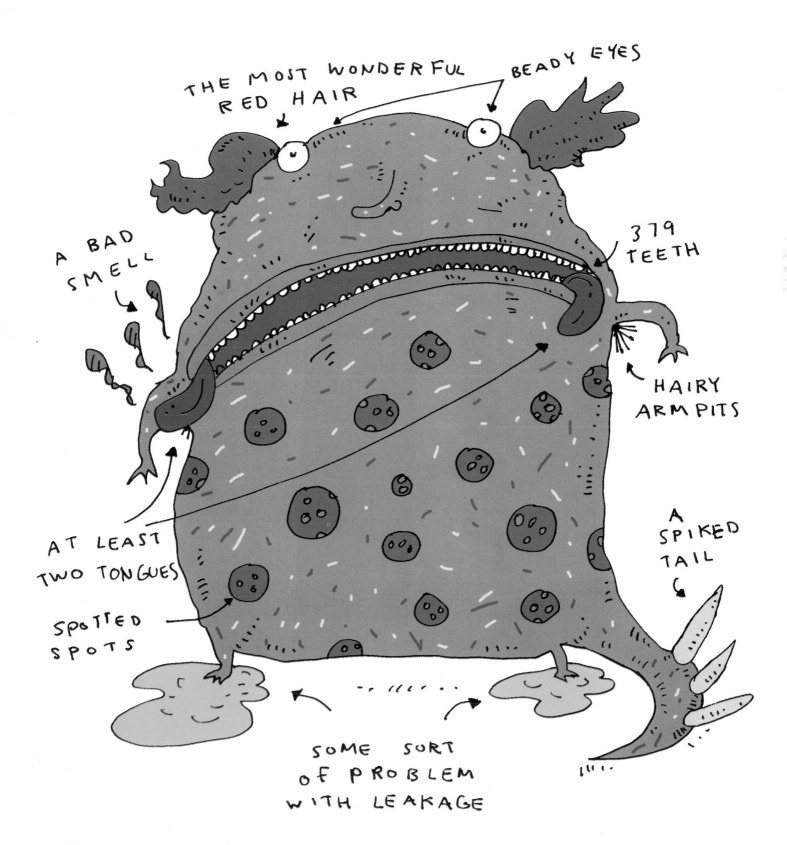

Whatever it was, the Something or Other certainly had no shame, because it proceeded to dance badly and to sing horribly off-key. "Your wish, your wish—tomorrow I will grant your wish!"

And as quickly as it had appeared, it was gone.

Joe Capri couldn't believe his eyes or his ears.

He was so excited, he couldn't even finish breakfast. "Jumpin' fuzzy lizards!" he bubbled.

HA HA Ha HA Ha
HA Ha Ha HA
Ha Ha Ha Ha
Ha Ha Ha HA HA
Ha Ha Ha HA HA
Ha Ha HA HA HA
Ha Ha HA HA HA HA
Ha Ha HA HA HA HA
Ha Ha HA HA HA HA
Ha Ha Ha HA HA HA
Ha Ha HA HA HA HA

HA!

Then Joe laughed long and hard at the
very thought of his wish being granted.

In just twenty-four hours Joe Capri would be young again. His legs wouldn't be tired, his skin wouldn't be wrinkled, and when he bent down, he wouldn't creak.

Joe was already entertaining the idea of trying out for the New York Yankees center field position.

With a bit more pep in his step, Joe shuffled out of his house and down to the corner. He hopped on the local bus and took it all the way across town to the home of his grandson, Michael Francis Capri.

When
they
saw
each other,
they
hugged.

Joe told his grandson about
his wish and the dancing, singing
Something or Other.

When it occurred to them
that the next day they could
be the same age, they laughed
themselves silly.

They went for a walk through the woods. Michael listened as his grandfather talked about how much he was looking forward to being young again.

Joe told Michael all about the
Marx Brothers,

and he taught him how to
make Harpo faces.

He demonstrated how to
skip stones on the lake.

He showed Michael
how to find his way out
of the woods without
a compass by using the
moss on the trees.

But mostly Joe talked about his wife, Michael's grandmother. "You would've loved her to bits," he whispered.

Michael thought
his grandfather
was magnificent.

That night Michael Francis Capri
couldn't sleep. He kept thinking
about his grandfather's tired legs,
his wrinkled skin, and how he
creaked when he bent down.

Finally, he couldn't stand it any longer. He threw off his blanket, went to his bedroom window, and wished on a star.

Michael wished that the dancing, singing Something or Other would not grant his grandfather's wish. He needed his grandfather to be his grandfather . . . just the way he was.

And on that very same night, on that very same star, Joe Capri made a wish, too. He wished he could change his wish.

Joe no longer wanted to be made young. He just wanted a lot more days with his grandson.

And just like that, Joe Capri and his grandson, Michael Francis Capri, *both* got their wishes.